To Ethan,

Happy birthday, #6!

Love Uncle Art
& Aunt Sabine

LITTLE LAKE
SAGA

NELSON MILLER
ILLUSTRATED BY KATHY BEDARD

CAITLIN
PRESS

Little Lake Saga
Copyright © 1996 by Nelson R. Miller
Illustrations copyright © 1996 by Kathy Bedard

Caitlin Press Inc.
P.O. Box 2387, Stn. B
Prince George, B.C.
V2N 2S6

Caitlin Press gratefully acknowledges the financial support of the Canada Council and the British Columbia Cultural Services Branch, Ministry of Tourism, Small Business and Culture.

Printed in Canada

Canadian Cataloguing in Publication Data

Miller, Nelson R., 1922-
  Little Lake saga

  ISBN 0-920576-58-3

  1. Natural history--Canada, Northern--Juvenile fiction. I.
Bedard, Kathy. II.Title.
PS8576.I54L57 1996   jC813'.54   C96-910229-1
PZ7.M63155Li 1996

The beauty and majesty of the far north has to be experienced; it cannot justly be described. I dedicate this small book to its inhabitants—all of them—animal, vegetable, mineral, and the unseen elements of nature's remarkable wisdom. So use the north, wander through its winter magic or just soak up your share of the summer splendour. Nurture it, guard it, pass it on to future generations that they might understand its place in the stream of life. The far north is the last of our natural frontiers. Be ever mindful to give back in plenty for the bounty you have received.

All the best to you and yours.
Keep on reading.
Nelson R. Miller.

In humble appreciation of my own indebtedness.

Nelson R. Miller
1996

Our far north is a wild and wonderful region of this ancient land. Its vast stretches of forests, lakes and meadows reach all the way to the great western mountains. A little lake is part of this wilderness. It nestles, almost unnoticed, in a small basin shoved up against the first rising foothills. It is separated from a much bigger lake by a rock shelf that forms a natural bridge between the forest and a small meadow. Animals cross here on their treks from the lowland timber to summer feeding grounds in the high country.

Almost in the center of the little lake an upcrop of rock and moss forms a small island. A few evergreens struggle to grow there. Tiny wavelets, pushed by the breeze, wash against the rock with hushed, rippling whispers. A gentle rain peppers the water and drips lazily through the small trees, from branch to branch, and soaks into the moss below.

Schools of little fish swim around the lake bottom near shore. Frogs jump in and out of the shallows and scramble for food among the ferns. Their sweet frog-song fills the summer evening.

On a wide stretch of sandy beach an old birch tree stands alone. No other trees have been able to take root in the rocky soil. Dragonflies zip among its flashing leaves. Round and round through the swirling branches, often skimming low over the water, they race and play their mating game.

Sadly, there are few other animals, and little plant growth, in the basin. Perhaps it's the shade from the nearby hills but the heavy ground cover of willow and brush surrounding other lakes has not sprung up here. But as summer draws to a close that is about to change.

An early autumn storm has been brewing for days, gathering together in the high country. Suddenly thunder and lightening ride out of the hills on the shoulders of huge, black rain clouds. A driving wind sweeps across the foothills and through the forest scooping up seeds and branches with its billowing breath. It roars down across the basin. The old birch, bent double again and again, manages each time to spring up like a soldier to its usual stand. Its branches clatter in a wild salute.

Then, as quickly as the storm arrived, it's gone, gusting out across the lowlands.

Tree cones and seeds of wildflowers, grasses and willow scattered by the storm, settle into every crack and crevice of the basin. Waterplant seeds and bull-rush down sink into the lake bottom and are quickly swallowed by the mud.

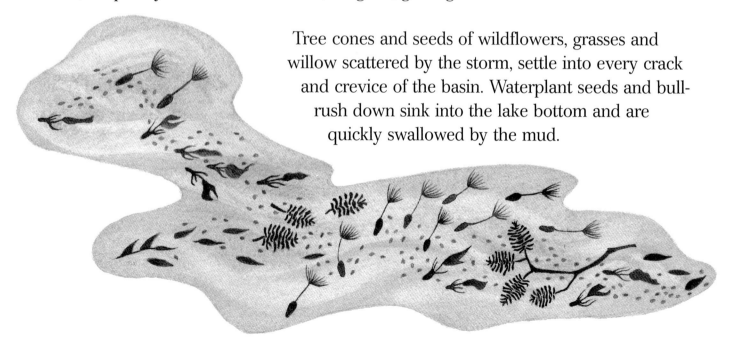

Soon after, the forest blaze of autumn gives way to winter. Ice, formed first in the shallows, moves out to cover the little lake. A solid freeze, before much snowfall, turns the lake into a giant mirror. The sun reflects off the ice like a huge fireball.

Trickles of melting snow are the first sign the long northern winter is over and spring is finally returning. The creek comes alive and recklessly cuts away the ice and snow in its path. It pours into the lake, melting the ice in a growing circle. The creek, wide as a small river now, overflows its highest banks and floods the meadow and the marshland near the foothills.

As the snow recedes dandelion and clover are the first of the new plants to show, followed by early buds of willow and brush. Shoots of bullrush and watergrass appear on the lake bottom like tiny crowns. Every day they grow higher until they poke above the water.

A pair of blackbirds, flying low, check out the new growth. Eventually, when the bull-rushes are mature and there are more of them, the blackbirds could return to nest. A sleek doe and her fawn stop on the rock shelf. The doe sniffs the air for danger. She smells the fresh grass and clover but, for now, the safety of higher ground is more important. Even the sky-flying hawk delays his flight to take a turn around the basin.

By late summer patches of grass, clover and brush are everywhere. Then autumn frosts colour the forest again, and soon snow is drifting across the lake ice. A cow moose and her long-legged calf crop the new alder and willow trees off at snow level. When the drifts get too high for the calf the pair move on to more sheltered groves deep in the forest.

Under the snow, field mouse and chipmunk families are snug in burrows tunnelled through the moss. Squawking ravens patrol overhead. Their search for food is never-ending and they miss nothing on their low swoops over the forest and meadow. An eagle, the flash of its white head and tail the only warning, circles in the cold sky. But the rodents are safe beneath the heavy drifts, and they have full storehouses close by.

When fierce storms bear down out of the north chick-a-dee, grosbeak and siskin shelter in the big spruce trees of the forest. The old birch, its branches bare and still, stands sentry alone in wintry splendor.

On mist-shrouded nights the northern lights rise up from their polar home. They shoot above the tallest trees and the highest mountains reaching for the north star and beyond. They sway and swirl in an unruly ballet to a musical score written on a frozen sky.

On the coldest nights the lake ice heaves and cracks with a sound like summer thunder. Trees snap and limbs fall. Nothing moves except the moon, marking its solitary journey past the stars.

Then the moonlight brings out the wolves, their gathering cries a chorus of warning. Dominant animals ahead, the pack streams off in line across the basin. Trails lead into the forest or up to the foothills. Tonight their prey fades into the thick underbrush of the forest and, silent now, the wolves give chase and disappear through the dark trees. The hunt is on.

Warm, southern breezes bring an early spring. The creek courses down from the high country and flows across the ice on the still-frozen lake. Spill-over floods the marsh even before the snow is gone.

Within weeks willow and alder buds are puffed up like brown beans. Tiny pine seedlings shove their heads up among the rocks and scrub, and soon tender green leaves are unfolding on the branches of the birch. The sky is filled with ducks and geese on a stopover to summer breeding grounds in the high north. They assemble in V formations, circling until each bird finds its place. Then they, and their wild cries, are gone.

Up in the foothills a bear and her cub, now in its second year, are ready to leave their winter den. The old bear has spent many winters here, under a rock overhang, protected by a large bluff. Last autumn, the bears had returned to the basin from a full summer foraging in the forest. After a final fattening up in the blueberry meadow, they added more leaves and branches to the big brush pile that made up the den. They are thin now, hungry, and drawn to the green sprouting in the lake clearing.

Later, stuffed with clover, the cub rolls on the beach. He shakes himself, flinging sand everywhere, and uses the trunk of the old birch for a scratching post.

One morning a pair of mallard ducks swoop in over the foothills and head immediately for the stand of bullrushes and watergrass. Food is plentiful here, and they spend the day feeding on the little lake, heads down, tails bobbing. At dusk they take cover in the meager vegetation on the little island.

The next day the young female and her colourful mate search out a safe place for their nest deep in the dense brush along the shore. They bring mud from the lake bottom, dry bullrush leaves, small willow branches and bits of brush, always approaching the secret site by a roundabout way. They make as little noise as possible. It's a good nest for their first effort, large and comfortable, lined with down and feathers plucked from their own bodies. Predators will have a hard time spotting the nest as they fly overhead or as they explore through the thick undergrowth.

A pair of robins have taken a liking to one of the old birch's high forked branches. They make a bowl-shaped framework of twigs and moss plastered with mud, an exact fit for their small shapes. The nest is hidden by leaves and as soon as it is finished, the female starts setting. In a few days there are five pale blue eggs. When the red-breasted male isn't foraging for food, he proudly sings from a higher limb.

Killdeer take turns on their nest, a hollow in the gravel so well-blended into the beach even close up you can't see the three eggs. When a coyote trots up the beach, one of the killdeer makes a frightened cry and limps away, dragging a wing. This imitation of a wounded bird lures the hunter from the nest and its precious eggs. Then just as the coyote springs to capture what it thinks is helpless prey, the killdeer takes flight, leaving the coyote surprised. And still hungry.

The bear and her cub have already left the basin and, when the flies get too bother-some in the open, the moose and deer leave too. Small flocks of ducks continue to fly in to feed on the little lake and the island but the mallards keep to themselves. There are seven dull green eggs in their nest now. The female cradles them under her body, keeping them at the right temperature and humidity. Periodically she rotates the eggs to keep the yolks perfectly centered. The male takes turns on the nest to let her feed and exercise.

The killdeer hatch first. They are soon scurrying after their parents, learning how to find food on their own along the water's edge. The basin echoes with their mournful cries.

You have to listen carefully to hear the faint chirping of the hungry, young robins. Mouths always open, they keep their parents busy bringing them caterpillars and other insects.

One day the mother duck waddles out of the brush with her seven little ones close behind. The father duck struts along, and they coax the babies into the water for their first swim. Soon the ducklings are flapping their small wings, trying to take off like the older birds. Every evening the family retreats to the safety of the brush. At dawn they are back on the water, practicing again. Summers are short in the far north.

Wildflowers are blooming. Blueberries are ripe. Red raspberries brighten the forest edge and the small clearings in the foothills. The breezes are sweet with the aroma of clover and the flowers. Tiny pines, just visible earlier, are shooting up. Even on the island, where the ducks gather to sun themselves on the warm rocks, the small trees are sporting fresh green growth.

The robins, almost naked at birth, have feathered out, made their solo flights and taken off. The killdeer are gone. And the ducklings, nearly full-grown, fly for the first time. The migrating ducks that went north in the spring return just before the first frosts. The sky fills with their familiar cries. The mallard family joins a gathering flock and is soon headed south.

The winter is hard, with light snowfalls compared to other years. The basin is bitterly cold. The hardy old bear, alone in her brush-lined den now that her cub has gone off on its own, awakes often during the coldest weeks and sniffs the air for a hint of spring.

When spring does arrive the basin shows the signs of a harsh winter. Willows in open areas are frost burned right down to ground level. The brush, usually protected by heavy snow, is damaged the most. Branch tips aren't leafing out. In fact, many branches are dead and break off in the first spring storm. Some bushes are completely destroyed and will never bloom again. The creek that normally overflows its banks at break-up has just enough water to top up the marsh and lake. There's no run-off this year.

Still, something is happening in the basin.

There's a new sound. A busy crashing and splashing. A young beaver pair is cutting down alder saplings and noisily dragging them through the marsh to the lakeshore.

Whenever a beaver lodge becomes too crowded and a new litter is due, the parents chase out older family members to fend for themselves. This is what had happened to these young beavers. On their own for the first time, they'd met several nights earlier on the shore of the big lake on the other side of the rock shelf. They'd been searching since then for a place to start their own lodge.

That first dawn they'd checked out the area surrounding the little lake. Because their sight works best underwater, it was their sensitive ears and noses that told them they'd found a safe place.

A low foothill, with plenty of young poplar and willow, sloped right down to the lake. On one side the marsh was almost overgrown with the right size alder. On the other the hill fell away gently to the meadow. Centered on the hill the yearly run-off had cut a ditch from part way up the slope down to the water. Near the lake one bank of the ditch had caved in over the years leaving a large indent. The beavers had chosen this site for their new home.

The beavers make many trips, over several days, falling trees and dragging them noisily through the marsh, to stockpile their building materials.

Once the female beaver catches a whiff of the old bear. She slaps the water hard with her tail, a sound that can be heard all over the basin, and warns her mate. He quickly leaves the alder tree he's gnawing and scurries to the safety of the lake.

The lodge begins against the caved in portion of the ditch. The beavers pile and cross-pile the poles and cement them together with mud from the bottom of the lake. It's a helter-skelter design, but effective at keeping out predators.

Slowly the lodge grows toward the lake and down into the water. Now the beavers work mostly at night. They feel safer in the dark. In the day they rest in burrows dug into the bank some distance from the lodge and connected by tunnels or trenches to deep reaches of the lake.

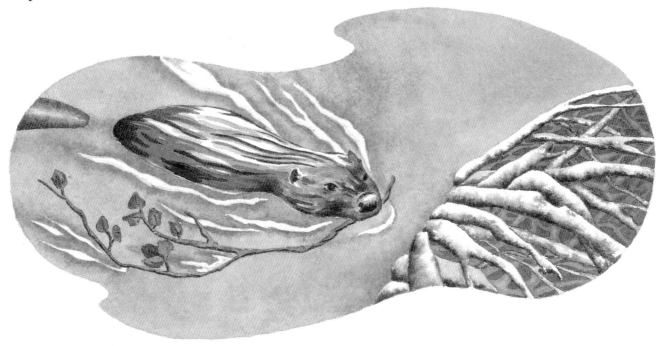

By mid-summer it's hard to see the damage done by winter's killing frosts. Everything is so green. Four pairs of ducks are nesting in the basin this year. Bears feed on the blueberries and occasionally moose leave the forest to browse in the marsh. The deer, keeping a safe distance from the bears, are back. There are five of them travelling together now, led by a proud buck. The fawn, almost full-grown, has lost its baby colours and is taking on the reddish coat of its mother.

The beaver lodge is nearly finished. The female has lined the floor of the living area with a carpet of slivered twigs. Excess water drains through this layer and runs off the clay below, keeping the den dry. Next spring, before her babies are born, the mother beaver will replace the carpet with a fresh nest of twigs chewed to fine, soft threads. Meanwhile she and her partner feast on waterlilies in the silver moonlight filtering through the leaves of the old birch.

The full moon, high above the mountains, draws the coyotes. The basin rings with their sharp, piercing barks as the scattered family members identify themselves. Gradually the pack merges on a hilltop in a frantic jangle of greeting. The jabber fades as they move out. The stars wink, playing their endless game with the night, and all is quiet in the basin.